CUENTO
DE LUZ

To you, reader, for allowing me into your heart.
- Carmen Gil -

Waterproof and tear resistant
Produced without water, without trees and without bleach
Saves 50% of energy compared to normal paper

Mister Yes
Text © 2017 Carmen Gil
Illustrations © 2017 Miguel Cerro
This edition © 2017 Cuento de Luz SL
Calle Claveles, 10 | Urb. Monteclaro | Pozuelo de Alarcón | 28223 | Madrid | Spain
www.cuentodeluz.com
Title in Spanish: Señor Sí
English translation by Jon Brokenbrow
Printed in PRC by Shanghai Chenxi Printing Co., Ltd. April 2018, print number 1632-2
2nd printing
ISBN: 978-84-16733-36-1

Carmen Gil / Miguel Cerro

Mr. Yes knew how to do lots of things. He knew how to make paper elephants that could wave their trunks. He knew how to do the trick where you push needles through balloons without making them pop. He beat everyone playing checkers. He could throw stones and make them skip twenty times over the water. He could say the trickiest tongue twisters ever:

"Peter Piper picked a peck of pickled peppers," he would say to all his friends. But the one thing Mr. Yes had never learned was to say "no."

Peter Piper picked a

One day, Mr. Yes was offered an ice cream made of humming bird poop and slug slime.

"Try it! It'll tickle your tongue!" they said.

"Well, I don't know … " said Mr. Yes. And even though it looked horrible, he couldn't say "no," and he ate the whole bowl. As you can imagine, he had a tummy ache for three whole days.

Mr. Yes crossed his arms and looked at himself in his bathroom mirror. He spoke to his reflection angrily.

"Why didn't you say no?" he asked. "I don't like you one little bit."

One afternoon, a salesman rang his bell. He had a huge suitcase, full of strange objects. There was a tennis racket without any strings, an owner's license for a cloud of steam, and a ten-pound can of invisible paint.

"My products are the very best, and the cheapest you'll ever find. Buy them, and you won't regret it."

"Well, I don't know …" said Mr. Yes.

Even though Mr. Yes didn't need any of the things the salesman had in his suitcase, he couldn't say "no." Before he realized, he'd already paid for an umbrella full of holes for sunny days, a broken telephone you could only use to talk to yourself, and a box full of silence, to use on noisy days.

Once he was alone, Mr. Yes went off to find the man in his bathroom mirror.

"Why didn't you say no?" he asked, angrily. "I don't like you at all!"

Another time, the grocer's son stopped Mr. Yes in the street.

"Come with me, and we'll have some fun," he said. "We're going to hide a rubber snake in the cauliflower at the supermarket. Or maybe we'll swap the sugar for salt in the coffee bar on the corner."

"Well, I don't know ..." Mr. Yes didn't like those kinds of naughty tricks. But he couldn't say no, and soon he found himself joining in.

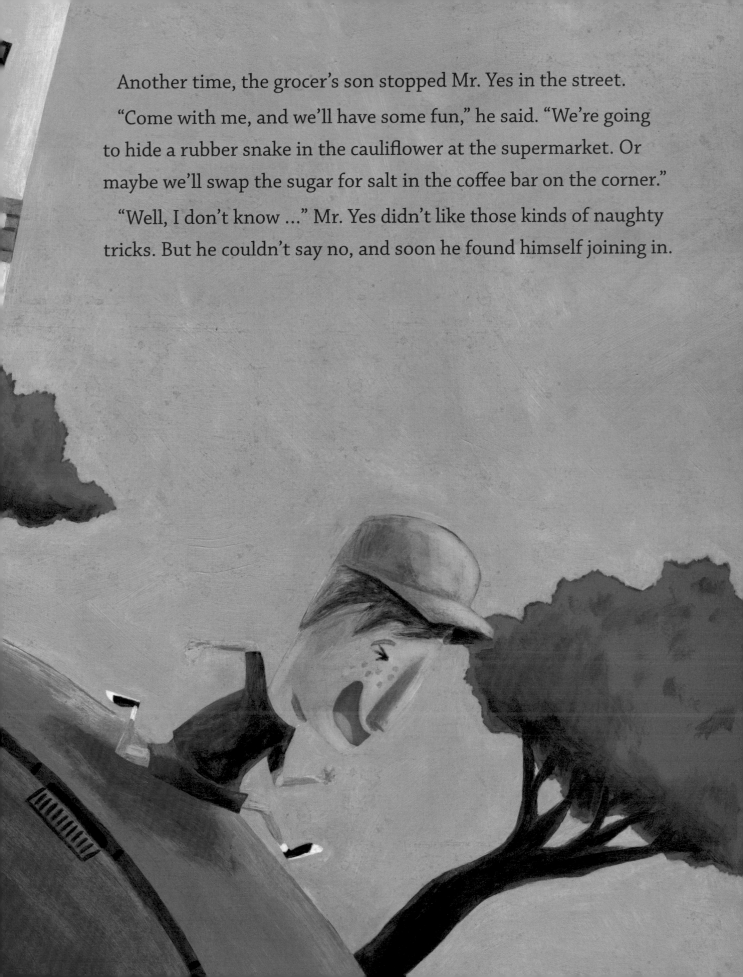

As soon as he got home, he ran upstairs and yelled at the face in his bathroom mirror.

"Why didn't you say no?" shouted Mr. Yes, who by now was incredibly angry. "I can't stand you."

Then, one sunny morning, Noah asked Mr. Yes to do some of his work, just like he had done many times before.

"Well, I don't know ..." muttered Mr. Yes.

He was convinced that Noah was taking advantage of him. But as he didn't know how to say "no," he had always accepted.

But just as he was about to reply, a fly buzzed into his open mouth and got stuck in his throat. All that came out was the first half of Noah's name:

"No."

"Well, okay then," said Noah. "If you don't want to ..." And he walked off, before Mr. Yes could get his voice back.

How much wood would a woodchuck chuck...

Mr. Yes started to feel as if thousands of brightly colored bubbles were bursting in his heart. A huge grin spread across his face, and he felt like he was walking on air. All the way home, he said his favorite tongue twister: "How much wood would a woodchuck chuck, if a wood chuck could chuck wood?"

As soon as he got home, he ran upstairs to see the man who lived inside his bathroom mirror. But now, he looked so handsome! So elegant! So friendly! And so, so charming.

"See how it wasn't so difficult?" whispered Mr. Yes. "You're the greatest!" And he tried to give him a kiss on the tip of his nose.

Mr. Yes knows how to do lots of things. He's an expert at building really high skyscrapers made out of soda cans. He's learned the trick where you pour water into a rolled up newspaper, and it turns into confetti. He's the city's tiddlywinks champion. He can throw paper balls into the trash can from the other side of the room. And he can still say tongue twisters faster than anyone else: "She sells sea shells on the sea shore!"

She sells sea shells on the sea shore!

And another thing: Mr. Yes knows how to say NO. He's realized that it comes in really handy: now he doesn't have to eat ice cream made out of humming bird poop, or buy umbrellas full of holes, or put rubber snakes in the cauliflower at the supermarket, or do his colleague's job for him ...

And if he does answer "YES," everyone's sure that he really, really means it. Like Charlotte, when she asked him:

"Would you like to come to my birthday party?"

"Yes!" he replied, in a clear voice, and with a great big grin on his face.

So does your friend—the one who lives in your bathroom mirror—know how to say NO? Well, if they don't, it's time you taught them. It's very easy. All you've got to do is wrinkle up your nose and purse your lips, just like you're going to give someone a kiss.